LUCY & TOM

From A to Z

Red Fox

RED FOX

UK | USA | Canada | Ireland | Australia | India | New Zealand | South Africa

Red Fox is part of the Penguin Random House group of companies
whose addresses can be found at global.penguinrandomhouse.com.

www.penguin.co.uk
www.puffin.co.uk
www.ladybird.co.uk

Penguin
Random House
UK

First published as *Lucy & Tom's ABC* by Victor Gollancz Ltd 1984
Published in paperback by Picture Puffins 1986
Published as *Lucy & Tom: From A to Z* 2018
001
Text and illustrations copyright © Shirley Hughes, 1984
The moral right of the author/illustrator has been asserted

Made and printed in China

A CIP catalogue record for this book is available from the British Library

ISBN: 978–1–782–95725–6

MIX
Paper from
responsible sources
FSC
www.fsc.org   FSC® C018179

Aa

Lucy and Tom know a lot of words beginning with a: a is for apples and ants; also for apricots, aunties, aeroplanes, acrobats and artists.

b is for **b**ooks and **b**ed. Lucy and Tom nearly always have a story read to them at bedtime. Tom knows most of his favourite stories by heart. When he's in bed he can look at the pictures and read aloud to himself. Lucy keeps some of her special books under her pillow, just in case.

Bb

Cc

c is for **c**ats, of course. Lucy and Tom's cat is called Mopsa. Her fur is brown with black stripes and patches of white. She doesn't often get cross or scratchy unless she's played with for just a bit too long.

c is for **c**olours and **c**rayons, too. It's fun mixing up the colours to make different ones.

Dd

d is for dogs. There are four living in Lucy and Tom's street. A little fluffy one, two middle-sized ones, and a big spotted one called Duchess. Tom doesn't like Duchess very much because she keeps knocking him over.

d is also for ducks who live on the lake in the park. Lucy and Tom often take them some bits of bread in a paper bag, and they come waddling up out of the water to be fed.

Ee

e is for **e**ggs, chocolate ones at Easter, all wrapped up in shiny paper, and real ones for breakfast. Lucy and Tom sometimes play a trick on Dad by putting an empty eggshell upside down in his egg cup. When he taps it, there's nothing inside. What a horrible surprise!

Ff

f is for **friends**. Lucy's best friend is Jane. They are in the same class at school and see each other every day. Tom's friends are James and Sam. They often play together. Sometimes they get cross with each other, but friends are important people so you can't be cross for long.

Gg

G is for **G**ranny and **G**randpa, two other very important people.

There are plenty of interesting things to do at Granny and Grandpa's house. Lucy helps Granny in the garden and Tom helps Grandpa mend things. They have some long talks together.

Hh

h is for **h**omes and **h**ouses.

Can you see where Lucy and Tom live?

Ii

i is for **ill**. This is Tom being ill in bed. He needs a lot of things to play with. Even then, he gets very hot and bored and keeps calling out for people to come and amuse him. Lucy is only a little bit ill. She's on the sofa, eating ice cream.

Jj

j is for **jumping**. Lucy has a skipping rope and she's learning to skip. She can get up to ten or even more. Tom can jump from the second stair, and from one paving stone to another. Sometimes he jumps on the furniture, too, though it's not really allowed.

Kk

k is for kites, flying high up over the windy hill.

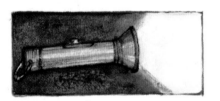

Ll

l is for light. There's sunlight, torchlight and twilight. There are street lights, car lights and the fairy lights on the Christmas tree. And there's the light that shines in from the landing when Lucy and Tom are asleep.

Mm

m is for **m**oon, the most magic light of all.

Nn
n is for **n**ursery school, where Tom spends his mornings.

Oo

o is for oranges and orange juice, which you can suck through a straw; o is also for oven. There are some good smells coming out of this one, but you have to be careful because it's VERY HOT.

Pp

p is for park and playing.

Qq

q is for queens, which is one of Lucy and Jane's favourite games. Tom is supposed to hold up their trains, but he doesn't often want to.

Rr

r is for **r**ooms. These are some of the rooms in Lucy and Tom's house.

Ss

s is for streets and shops. Lucy and Tom have been to the supermarket with Mum. They've bought something else beginning with s. Can you guess what it is?

Tt t is for **t**oys, **t**eatime and **t**elevision.

Uu
u is for **u**mbrellas.

Vv

v is for **v**oices. You can whisper in a very soft, tiny voice, like this, or you can shout in a VERY LOUD, NOISY VOICE, LIKE THIS, or you can make music with your voice by singing a tune. There are cross voices and kind voices, high voices and deep voices, happy voices and whiny voices.
Which kind of voice do you like best?

Ww

w is for **w**inter when it's too cold to play outside. The windows have frost on them and the water is frozen over.

When the snow comes, all the world is white.

Xx

x is for xylophone. Lucy's xylophone has eight notes and each one makes a different sound when you strike it. You write notes in a special way like this:

Yy

y is for **y**achts on the water and **y**achtsmen on the shore.

Zz

z is for zoo, of course.

z is also the end of the alphabet, and this is the
end of Lucy and Tom's abc.

AaBbCcDdEeFfGgHhIiJjKkLlMmNn
OoPpQqRrSsTtUuVvWwXxYyZz

Lollipop
and
Grandpa
and the
Christmas Baby

Penelope Harper

I   nes

Lollipop and her family are just sitting down to tea,
when Mum suddenly asks:
"How would you feel about a new baby brother or sister?"

"Ooooh!
Yes,please,"
says James.

Lollipop looks carefully at Mum, and then at Dad.

Hmmmmmmmmm.

"Do you understand what they're saying, James?"
says Lollipop. "It's already happening."

"The MOST exciting news," says Dad,
"is that the baby will be born
in time for Christmas.
It'll be the best Christmas present ever!"

"B-b-but I was going to ask
Father Christmas for a bike,"
says Lollipop.

As the weather starts to get colder,
Mum's tummy starts to get
bigger and **bigger**.

At first, Lollipop
thought she had
a melon up her
jumper . . .

then a football . . .

and now, a huge,
inflatable beach ball.

Lollipop knows three things
about babies:
They cry, most of the time.

They smell really, really stinky.

But worst of all . . .

. . . everybody loves them.

Christmas is **ruined!**

"Nonsense!" cries Grandpa.
"With everybody else busy getting ready
for the baby, you and I have got a
lot of work to do."

"First, we need the tallest, most stupendous Christmas tree we can find."

"This one is perfect,"
beams Lollipop.

"Brilliant work!" exclaims
Grandpa, his nostrils flaring,
and snowflakes sticking to
his moustache.

Grandpa sizes up the living room.
"The tree is a good start, but this
whole place could do with a little
bit of sprucing up.

"Why don't we make our very own Winter Wonderland?"

Yippeeeeeeeeee!

"We can't do that, Grandpa," sighs Lollipop, shaking her head. "We'd be f-f-f-frozen.

"How about we make some paper chains and some pom-poms, and use anything sparkly we can find?"

"What a tremendous idea!" cries Grandpa.

By Christmas Eve, all the decorations are finished,
and the house looks spectacular.

Dad helps Mum get her coat on.

"Lollipop, the baby is coming, so we have to go to the hospital. We're leaving you and Grandpa in charge."

"Righty-ho!" shouts Grandpa, leaping into action. "There's still plenty to do. We had better make sure Father Christmas can get down the chimney tonight."

WHOOOOOOSH!

"Whoops-a-daisy! That's gone right up my nose!"

"What about stockings?" asks Lollipop.

"Good thinking!" cries Grandpa, rummaging through the washing basket. "These should do the trick."

By the time they are finished, Grandpa is so tired he falls asleep.

It's Christmas morning and...

Father
Christmas
has been!

But Mum and Dad still aren't home.

Lollipop and Grandpa put on their coats and hats, and go and play in the snow.

Then they sing some carols (badly).

They even roast some chestnuts.

But Mum and Dad **still** aren't home.

"We'll just have to crack on with the
Christmas dinner," announces Grandpa.
They inspect the enormous turkey.
It's frozen solid.

"I'm not much of a cook," says Grandpa,
"but I know it needs to be warmer than that."

Grandpa paces the room, deep in thought.
"Maybe we had better stick to sandwiches," suggests Lollipop.

Lollipop and Grandpa set to work.

They make . . .

ham sandwiches with crisps in them . . .

cheese on cocktail sticks . . .

pickled onions . . .

and Grandpa makes the biggest knickerbocker glory

that Lollipop has **ever** seen!

They're just putting the finishing touches to the sausage and custard trifle, when . . .

"Wow!" gasps Mum.

"Incredible!" gulps Dad.

The Christmas Baby is all bundled up in a blanket.
He has teeny-tiny little hands, and teensy-weensy
little feet. He's very soft and warm, and . . . he's not crying!

Grandpa makes cups of tea for everyone, and Lollipop and James open their presents.

"This present should be for the baby,"
says Lollipop.
"After all, it's his birthday too!"

Suddenly, the doorbell rings.

Bing-Bong!

It's a photographer
from the local newspaper,
who's come to take a
picture of the
Christmas Baby.

Mum says to the photographer,
"Maybe my very grown-up little girl
should hold the baby in the picture."

Lollipop takes the
Christmas Baby very
carefully.
He grips her finger
really tightly.

Lollipop whispers to him,
"Welcome to the best Christmas ever!"

Merry Christmas everyone!